Secret Kingdom

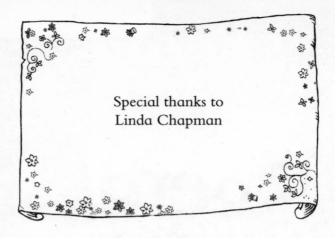

Special thanks to
Linda Chapman

ORCHARD BOOKS

First published in Great Britain in 2014 by Orchard Books
This edition published in 2016 by The Watts Publishing Group

3 5 7 9 10 8 6 4

© 2014 Hothouse Fiction Limited
Illustrations © Orchard Books 2014

A CIP catalogue record for this book is available from the British Library.

ISBN 978 1 40832 901 6

Printed in Great Britain by Clays Ltd, St Ives plc

Orchard Books
An imprint of Hachette Children's Group
Part of The Watts Publishing Group Limited
Carmelite House, 50 Victoria Embankment, London EC4Y 0DZ

An Hachette UK Company
www.hachette.co.uk
www.hachettechildrens.co.uk

Series created by Hothouse Fiction
www.hothousefiction.com

Magic Seal

ROSIE BANKS

ORCHARD

This is the Secret Kingdom

Snowy Seas

Contents

No More School!

"Hold on tight!" called Summer as she pushed Ellie and Jasmine on the roundabout at Honeyvale Park.

"Faster!" squealed Jasmine.

Summer gave the roundabout one last big push and jumped on too. Jasmine whooped as they all spun around.

Looking up at the blue sky Summer laughed, feeling as though they would keep spinning round for ever, but gradually the roundabout got slower and finally stopped completely.

Jasmine jumped off. "I love roundabouts!"

"Me too," Ellie said happily.

"Do you know what they remind me of?" Summer asked.

"I bet I can guess!" Ellie looked around, but there was no one close enough to hear.

"Whizzing off to the Secret Kingdom?" she whispered.

Summer nodded. "Yes!"

The three friends often visited a magic land called the Secret Kingdom. It was ruled by a jolly king called King Merry, and lots of amazing magical creatures like elves and unicorns lived there. Whenever they went to the Secret Kingdom, King Merry's Royal Pixie, Trixi, whisked the girls away in a sparkling cloud that spun them round and round – just like the roundabout, but a hundred times better!

"I hope we get another message from the Secret Kingdom soon," said Jasmine. "Half term would be the perfect time to have some more adventures as we'll be spending lots of time together anyway."

Ellie's green eyes sparkled. "You're right, although any time is the perfect time to have an adventure!"

"I think we should go back to my house and check the Magic Box," said Summer. "Another message might be waiting for us."

King Merry had invented a magical box that sent the girls a riddle whenever they were needed in the kingdom. Usually it was because the king's wicked sister, Queen Malice, was up to no good. She was determined to cause trouble until the Secret Kingdom was hers!

The girls ran to pick up their school bags and then set off for Summer's house.

"No more school for a week," said Jasmine happily, practising a pirouette as they walked.

Ellie grinned. "I bet I know what the elves learn at their school in the Secret Kingdom."

"What?" Summer asked.

"The *elf*-abet of course!" Ellie said.

Summer and Jasmine both groaned. Ellie giggled. "Come on!" she said, breaking into a run. "Race you back!"

Mrs Hammond, Summer's mum, opened the front door. "Hi, girls! How was your last day at school? There's lemonade in the fridge and I've made some fresh popcorn for you."

"Thanks, Mum," said Summer. "Can we take it upstairs?"

"Sure," her mum replied.

Summer, Ellie and Jasmine carried the drinks and the bowl of popcorn upstairs. The window was open and they could hear Summer's younger brothers playing outside in the garden. Summer's room was covered with posters of animals. There were lots of books stacked up on two shelves and a white fluffy rug on the floor. A little black cat was curled up on her bed.

Summer ran over and gave the cat a

kiss. "Hi, Rosa!"

Rosa purred and Summer stroked
her soft coat. "I'm surprised you're not
outside in the garden. You seem to like
my bed a lot at the moment."

Rosa rubbed her head against
Summer's hand. Three charms jingled
together on her collar.

Jasmine gently touched
the shimmering charms.
One was shaped like
a heart, one like a
flower and the last
was shaped like
a crown.

"The Animal Keepers' magic charms,"
she said softly. "We must get them back
to the three missing Keepers before
any more damage is done in the Secret
Kingdom."

The three girls looked serious for a
moment as they all remembered what
had happened in the Secret Kingdom the
last time they had been there.

Once every hundred years, kind King
Merry used the Secret Spellbook to
summon four Animal Keepers from a
magical shield. The Keepers were a
puppy, a seal, a bird and a lion cub
and their job was to magically travel
around the Secret Kingdom, spreading
fun, kindness, friendship and courage as
they went. After they had travelled all
the way around the land, the Keepers

returned to their shield for another
hundred years.

Just a few days ago, the girls had gone
to the Secret Kingdom to watch the
Animal Keepers being summoned and to
join in the celebrations. But something
awful had happened… Queen Malice
had put a curse on the Animal Keepers!
Instead of bringing kindness, courage,
friendship and fun, they would now
bring the opposite wherever they went
– meanness, cowardice, squabbling and
misery.

The Animal Keepers' magical charms
had been left behind when the animals
disappeared off around the kingdom,
and Summer had put them on Rosa's
collar for safekeeping. The three friends
had already managed to find one of the

Animal Keepers – the Puppy Keeper –
and as soon as they had reattached the
charm to his collar the puppy had been
freed from the queen's curse. But the seal,
lion and bird were still under her wicked
spell! King Merry had promised to send
the girls a message as soon as he and
Trixi had worked out where the missing
Animal Keepers were. Then Summer,
Ellie and Jasmine could try and return
their charms to them.

"Where's the Magic Box?" Ellie asked.

Summer pulled out a bag from under
her bed. "Here." She eased the box out
of the bag. The box was carved with
unicorns and mermaids and studded with
gems. The lid was a shimmering mirror.

Jasmine took it from Summer and
stroked its wooden sides. "I hope we get

another message soon—" She stopped
with a gasp. The whole box had begun
to shine and glow! "Oh, wow!" she
gasped. "Look!"

Golden words swirled across the
mirrored lid of the box. Her heart
beating fast, Summer jumped up and
shut the door. She didn't want anyone
coming in!

Ellie read the words out:

"The Animal Keeper that you seek,
Is near an ocean cold and deep.
To find her quickly you must go
To a land of ice and snow!"

There was a bright flash and the lid of
the box flew open. A map floated out
of one of the six compartments inside.

As the box shut again, the map hovered between the girls and unfolded itself, showing a moving picture of the Secret Kingdom. Flags waved from the pink turrets of the Enchanted Palace, unicorns cantered through green meadows and bubblebees hummed around Bubble Volcano. The map rustled slightly as if it was inviting the girls to look closer.

Summer, Ellie and Jasmine looked at each other in excitement. Another adventure was about to begin!

Snowy Seas

"Where do you think we have to go this time?" Ellie said. Whenever the girls got a message, the first thing they had to do was solve the riddle and work out where in the Secret Kingdom it meant.

"I'm not sure," said Jasmine doubtfully.

Ellie looked at the top of the map where there was a picture of a shield divided into quarters. It looked just like the Keepers' Shield that was kept in King

Merry's palace. In one quarter of the shield there was a silhouette of a puppy. Two of the other quarters were misty and unclear, but the final quarter was glowing with a strange bright light.

She looked closer. There was no animal in the picture, but there was a shimmering silhouette where the Keeper should be and they could see snowflakes falling and ice crystals forming around the edges of the picture. "Do you think this is another clue?" Ellie said.

"The riddle says we have to look for somewhere cold with an ocean," said Jasmine. "Maybe the shield is giving us a clue that it's somewhere snowy, too?"

"What about up here?" said Summer. She had been scanning the map and now she pointed to the north where there were snow-covered mountains, pine forests and a vast expanse of snowy land. Around the edge of the land was a dark sea with ice floes floating in it. It looked very cold indeed!

"Snowy Seas," Ellie said, reading out a small label to the side of the picture.

"I bet that's the answer to the riddle!" said Jasmine.

The three girls put their hands on the box and called out: "Snowy Seas!"

There was a bright flash and the lid of

the box flew open again, this time with
a tinkle of bells. In a flash of sparkles, a
tiny pixie flew out on a green leaf.

"Trixibelle!" cried Summer. Trixi
swooped around their heads and came to
a stop, hovering just above the map. She
was wearing a pink coat trimmed with
fake fur, cosy pink boots and
a fur-trimmed pink hat
was perched on her
blonde hair.

"Hello, girls!"
she said in
her silvery
voice.
"Are you
ready for
another
adventure?"

"Oh, yes!" Ellie, Summer and Jasmine cried.

"Good," Trixi said, looking relieved. "Because the animals near the Snowy Seas seem really unhappy. I'm sure it's something to do with one of the Animal Keepers. King Merry and I think one of them must have travelled there and their mixed-up magic is causing trouble. We really need you to come and help!"

Summer looked carefully at the shield on the map. "The shape on the snowy bit of the shield *does* look like a seal," she said thoughtfully. "And the Seal Keeper looks after kindness."

"We should go and talk to the ice mermaids who live in the Snowy Seas," said Trixi. "They help look after all the animals and magical creatures in that part of the Secret Kingdom. Maybe they'll know what's going on. Are you ready to go?"

"Yes!" they all cried.

Jasmine had a sudden thought. "What about warm clothes, Trixi? It looks very cold by the Snowy Seas. Should we get some coats and gloves?"

Trixi's green eyes twinkled. "Don't worry about that. I'll use my magic to make sure you're dressed in lovely, snuggly clothes."

The girls exchanged excited looks. They loved it when Trixi used her magic to give them new outfits!

Jasmine took Summer and Ellie's hands. "Then let's go!"

"No, wait," said Summer suddenly. She ran over to scoop up Rosa who gave a surprised miaow. "We need to take Rosa too. She's got the Keepers' charms on her collar!"

Summer carried Rosa over to join the others. Rosa gave Trixi an interested look but she didn't struggle or try to jump down. She seemed to know she was going to the Secret Kingdom again!

Trixi tapped the ring on her finger and called out:

*"Magic, please, we need to go
To where the sea meets ice and snow!"*

Silver sparkles whooshed out of the ring, surrounding the girls in a glowing cloud. They felt themselves being picked up and spun round and round in the air. Where were they going to land?

Ellie gasped as she found herself sitting
on a soft padded seat. The sparkles
cleared and the air suddenly filled with
the tinkling of bells and the soft thudding
of hooves.

"We're in a sleigh!" Jasmine realised.

"And look what's pulling us!"
exclaimed Summer in delight. A beautiful
white horse with feathery wings was

pulling the sleigh across a snowy
meadow. Summer saw that her school
uniform had vanished and she was now
wearing a snug yellow jacket with a
furry hood. She touched her head and
looked round at the others. Yes! They
all had their beautiful tiaras on too!
The tiaras appeared whenever the girls
came to the Secret Kingdom and showed
everyone that they were Very Important
Friends of King Merry.

Ellie was wearing a woolly purple jacket with matching boots and Jasmine was wrapped up in a glittery dark-pink scarf and matching gloves. Even Rosa had a warm jacket and matching boots to protect her paws from the snow! She sniffed at the boots curiously and then looked at Summer. Summer kissed her head. "Don't worry, you'll get used to them!" She was delighted that Rosa was joining them on another adventure in the Secret Kingdom!

The horse whinnied.

"Snowflake is saying hello," said Trixi. She had landed her leaf on the front of the sleigh and turned to face the girls, who were all sitting on the seat together. "He's a flying horse."

"He's beautiful," breathed Summer.

The horse's wings were folded along his back as he cantered across the snow.

"This place is amazing," said Jasmine, looking around at the landscape they were racing through. Everywhere sparkled and glittered, the ice and snow shining in the sunlight. They left the snowy meadow and galloped into a forest of pine trees. Immediately the scent of pine needles filled the air.

It was darker among the trees and very peaceful. White squirrels scampered up the tall tree trunks. A silver fox with big pointed ears ran alongside them before stopping and waving a paw as they whizzed on their way.

But just then, Jasmine spotted something that made her gasp. "What's that?"

Standing amongst the trees was a huge figure standing on two legs. He had thick white fur covered with a layer of frost and coal-dark eyes under big bushy white eyebrows.

"That's an ice giant," said Trixi. "Ice giants have magical powers. They can make ice with their hands and create any shape from it. They help keep this part of the kingdom cold and icy."

"He looks a bit scary!" said Summer.

"Don't worry. Ice giants are very kind," said Trixi. "They just don't see many other people out here!"

Snowflake whinnied and surged forwards, galloping out of the trees. His large wings unfurled and he leaped into the air, carrying them up into the blue sky.

"We're flying!" cried Jasmine. "Wheeee!"

Ellie didn't like heights and clutched the seat nervously, but the horse flew

smoothly and with Jasmine and Summer
on either side of her, Ellie soon realised
she was perfectly safe.

Snowflake flew across the plain,
heading towards the sea at the edge
of the land. When they reached it, he
flew down and landed beside a shining
palace made of ice. Its walls glittered and
its turrets were decorated with starfish
carved from ice. The
palace was built right
on the edge of the
land and its walls
plunged down
into the sea.

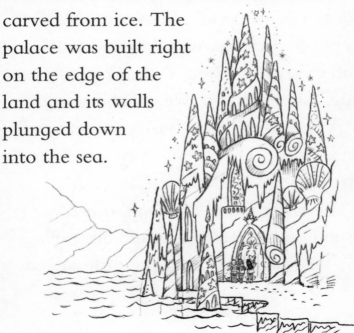

"This is Lady Frida's palace," said Trixi. "Lady Frida is the ruler of the ice mermaids. Her palace goes all the way down to the bottom of the ocean. Most of the rooms are under the water but sometimes the ice mermaids like to come up to the higher levels and be close to the land."

She flew up on her leaf and the girls got out of the sleigh. Summer went over to pat Snowflake, who lowered his head and nuzzled her hair. "Thank you for the ride," she told him. He snorted softly.

"You can go home now, Snowflake," said Trixi. "Thank you very much for bringing us here."

The horse tossed his head, turned round and cantered into the air, pulling the sleigh behind him. The girls waved and then turned back to the castle. The door loomed before them. It was carved with mermaids and shells. "Shall we just knock on it?" asked Jasmine, spotting a big brass knocker in the shape of a fish.

Trixi nodded. Jasmine walked forward and took hold of the knocker. She banged it several times and waited. But no one came.

"That's strange," said Trixi. "Maybe the ice mermaids are all in the underwater rooms. We could swim down and see."

Summer looked at the dark sea. It looked very cold and she really didn't like going underwater. "Do...do we have to?" she said uncertainly. "It looks freezing."

Trixi kissed her cheek. "Don't worry. If I use a bit of magic then you won't feel the cold at all and you'll be able to swim really well. Of course, it will mean turning into something else…"

"Turning into what?" asked Ellie, alarmed.

Trixi grinned. "Into mermaids, of course!"

Memaid Magic

The girls stared at Trixi.

"Can you really turn us into mermaids?" asked Jasmine, amazed.

Trixi nodded. "Just for a short time. My magic will let you understand all the underwater animals, too."

"But what about Rosa?" Summer said anxiously. We can't leave her behind."

"Of course not! She can come with us," said Trixi.

"You'll turn her into a mermaid too?" Summer said in astonishment.

"No." Trixi smiled. "But I'll give her a comfortable, dry way to travel. Bring her to the water's edge and I'll show you."

They all slipped and slid across the snow until they were standing right beside the water's edge. Trixi tapped her ring and called out a spell:

*"Magic ring, a bubble form,
To keep Rosa snug and warm!"*

A silvery bubble popped into the air, surrounding Rosa. "Miaow!" the little cat said, surprised. Rosa sat down cautiously, her eyes wide. The bubble bobbed up in the air. It had a silver string attached to it. Trixi took one

end and handed
it to Summer.

"You'll
need to hold
tight so she
doesn't
float off
when we go
underwater.
Now, it's
time for some
magic for the
rest of us! Sit
down, girls."

Ellie, Summer and
Jasmine shrugged at one another as they
sat down on the slippery ice. Jasmine felt
a tingle of excitement.

Trixi tapped her ring again.

"Mermaids now we want to be,
So we can swim under the sea!"

A cloud of multicoloured sparkles flew out of the ring and streamed towards the girls. They surrounded their toes and then whirled up around their bodies. Ellie, Summer and Jasmine felt their skin tingling and warmth rushed through them from their toes to the top of their heads. It was a very strange feeling. With a pop, the sparkles vanished.

"Oh, wow!" cried Ellie.

Instead of legs, they all now had long shining tails covered with shimmering scales! Ellie's tail was lilac and dark purple, Summer's was blue and silver and Jasmine's was different shades of pink.

Even Trixi, sitting on her leaf, had a tiny tail that shimmered emerald green and gold. They were wearing pretty long-sleeved tops that matched their tail colours.

"Look at my tail!" said Jasmine, waving it from side to side.

Trixi grinned. "Just wait to see how well you can swim with it. Dive in!"

Putting her arms above her head, Trixi dived neatly from her leaf into the water. The girls followed her, with Summer holding on tightly to the string attached to Rosa's waterproof bubble.

The girls swished their tails and whizzed through the water. The sea didn't feel cold at all now that they were mermaids! Jasmine turned a somersault and Ellie twirled round and then dived deeper before shooting back up. It was the most amazing feeling.

"Come on! Follow me!" called Trixi,
tiny bubbles coming out of her mouth as
she spoke.

The friends swam down and down.

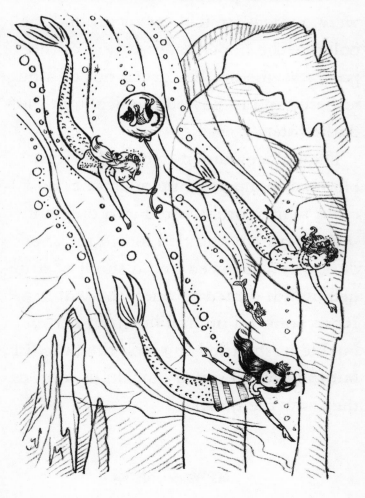

The water changed from turquoise to deep blue but they found they could still see clearly. As they got closer to the bottom of the ocean, they saw that there were gardens stretching out around the palace. The underwater section of the palace seemed to be carved out of a huge iceberg, and it glowed magically in the dark waters.

The palace gardens were filled with blue sea sponges, white anemones and curly white coral twisted into different shapes. An icy path led into a forest of dark green seaweed and a shoal of stripy, yellow fish darted through the water. Rosa bounced up and down in her bubble as she tried to reach the little fish, but they swam away quickly as soon as they saw the girls.

A moment later, a silvery octopus poked its head out of a cave. But when the girls swam closer he shot off in a panic, leaving behind a cloud of bubbles.

"That's odd," said Trixi. "It's as if the creatures here think we are going to do something horrible to them. But why would they think that?"

Just then, Jasmine heard a low, ghostly moaning noise. "What's that?" she asked, spinning round to look behind them.

"It's coming from over there." Summer looked towards the seaweed forest. She handed Ellie Rosa's bubble string and swam over to the forest. She peered through the tall grasses and gasped. There, making the crying, moaning sound, was a shimmering baby whale! He was a bluey-white colour, blending in perfectly with the icy waters around him. His big green eyes sparkled sadly.

"Oh, you poor thing," said Summer, swimming up to the whale. Even though he was a baby, he was still much bigger than Summer! "What's the matter?" she asked kindly.

"The ice mermaids made me get lost!" the baby whale cried, tears welling up in his big green eyes.

Ellie, Jasmine and Trixi came over too.

"What do you mean?" Trixi asked. "Ice mermaids are *never* mean to sea creatures."

"Well, these ones were," said the whale sadly. "I asked them to help me find my mum but they took me into the deep caves instead. My mum wasn't there and now I'm lost! The mermaids lied!"

Summer hugged him. "That wasn't very nice."

"And very unlike them!" said Trixi, looking worried.

"It sounds like the seal *must* be the Animal Keeper that's around here, and her mixed-up magic is making the mermaids mean instead of kind," said Jasmine. "We *really* need to talk to the mermaids to find out where the seal has gone now."

"We need to help you, too," Summer said to the whale. "What's your name?"

"Arva," he told her.

"Well, I'm Summer and this is Ellie, Jasmine and Trixi, and my cat Rosa. We'll help you find your mum, Arva. I bet she's worried about you too."

"You know lots about animals, Summer," said Ellie. "How can we let Arva's mum know he's here?"

Summer thought for a moment.
"Have you tried calling for her in a
way she'll know it's you, Arva? I know
whales talk to each other using echoey
calls and cries."

"I have tried calling her," said Arva.
"But I'm not loud enough."

Jasmine looked at Trixi. "Could you
help, Trixi? Could you make Arva's
voice louder with your magic?"

"I think so," said Trixi. "Let me see…"
She tapped her ring and called out a
spell:

"Arva's voice now amplify.
Let his mother hear his cry."

"Try again!" Ellie said eagerly to the
whale.

Arva opened his mouth and made the
low sound again. It was so loud this time
that the girls had to cover their ears!

There was a pause.

"Mum!" Arva said suddenly "I'm sure
I can hear her!" The girls hadn't heard
anything.

"Try again," urged Summer.

Arva called to his mother again.

As the girls uncovered their ears, they heard a faint answering call.

Arva swam round in an excited circle. "It *is* her! It's worked!"

Moments later, a huge shimmering whale came swimming slowly through the forest, looking anxiously from side to side. Trixi tapped her ring to return Arva's voice to normal.

"Mum! I'm here!" Arva called, racing towards her.

His mother gave a whistle of delight and rubbed noses with him. "Oh, Arva. Where have you been?"

The baby whale explained. "These mermaids helped me find you! They made my voice louder."

Arva's mother bowed her great head and seemed to shimmer even more

brightly as she smiled at the girls.
"Thank you for being so kind to my
son. I hope one day we will be able to
do something to help you in return," she
said. She turned to her baby. "Come
now, Arva. And this time, stay close
to me!" Arva and his mother swam off
together happily.

The girls beamed at one another and
then swam on, trying to find an ice
mermaid to speak to. As they swam,
Summer noticed that a soft glow was
coming from the heart-shaped charm on
Rosa's collar. She could see a few words
starting to appear, but before she could
show the other girls, Jasmine reached
the underwater walls of the palace and
found another door with a knocker. She
knocked it sharply.

A few moments passed
and then the door
opened. A mermaid
looked out.
She was very
beautiful, with
long dark hair
and a turquoise
tail, but her face
was cross. "We don't
want any visitors today!"
she snapped. "Go away!"
Then she shut the door in Jasmine's face!

Jasmine blinked. "Well, that wasn't
very friendly."

"Knock again!" Trixi urged.

Jasmine did. The door flew open.

"What part of 'Go away!' don't you
understand!" snapped the mermaid. She

went to shut the door again.

"Please, wait!" cried Trixi. "We need to talk to Lady Frida!"

"Not today!" shouted the mermaid and she slammed the door.

The girls and Trixi stared at each other, and then swam away from the palace, resting on the sea bed a little way off.

"We know the Seal Keeper's mixed-up magic is the thing that's making the mermaids unkind," said Ellie. "But I don't understand why all the other creatures down here aren't being unkind too?"

"I think the seal must have swum directly through the palace," said Trixi. "But if the seal does come face-to-face with the other creatures, then they'll become unkind too!"

Summer looked thoughtfully at the
heart-shaped charm dangling from
Rosa's collar. She could now read the
words that had appeared:

"If you want to summon me..."

"Look!" she said, showing her friends.
"In our last adventure with the Puppy
Keeper, when all the words appeared
on the charm we were able to call the
puppy to us. I think that by being kind
to the baby whale, we made some of the
words appear on *this* charm!"

"We need to make more of the spell
appear," Ellie said thoughtfully. "Maybe
we could start by doing something nice
for the ice mermaids. Then perhaps
they'll see that we are here to help."

"Why don't we pick them some sea flowers?" suggested Jasmine, swimming over to a pretty patch of seaweed dotted with flowers that sparkled like sapphires.

"That's a good idea!" agreed Trixi. "I'll use my magic to make sure that more flowers grow back right away."

The girls picked a bunch of the sparkling sea flowers and went back to the large doors of the palace. Ellie knocked on the door.

A few moments later, the same mermaid opened the door. She looked even crosser than before. "You again! What do you want?" she shouted.

"We wanted to give Lady Frida these flowers—" began Summer, but before she could finish, the rude mermaid had grabbed the flowers from her hand and

thrown them onto the sea floor!

"That's it!" snarled the ice mermaid. "I've had enough of this. I'll have to *make* you go away!" And with that, she swam directly at the girls with her arms outstretched and a fierce look in her eyes!

The Pingaloos

Ellie, Summer, Jasmine and Trixi swam quickly up to the surface, pursued by the angry mermaid. They'd never swum so fast! The mermaid bobbed up to the surface a little way away and shook her fist at the friends. "Now stay away!" she snapped, before diving back underwater.

"Phew, I'm glad she didn't catch us!" panted Summer as Rosa bobbed next to her in her bubble. The little cat looked like she had enjoyed the underwater race! "But that plan definitely didn't work."

The girls saw the walls of the ice palace glittering against the blue sky and the snowy land stretching away in all directions.

Just then, Ellie heard a squawking noise to their left and turned. "Whoa!" she gasped. "Look over there!"

A giant ice floe was floating across the ocean. It was covered with birds that looked like penguins, only instead of being black and white, they were all the colours of the rainbow! They had big bushy eyebrows, striped beaks and sleek feathers. They waddled around, calling out to each other. "Pingalooo!" they cried. "Pingalooo!" In the centre of the floe was a cluster of brightly coloured little igloos that were obviously the birds' homes. They kept popping in and out of the doors and calling to one another.

"What kind of birds are they?" asked Summer in amazement.

"They're pingaloos," said Trixi.

"They're called that because of the sound they make. They live on the ice floes in the Snowy Seas."

"Are they using paddles?" asked Jasmine, staring. A team of pingaloos were all holding big long-handled paddles. They were using them to push the ice floe through the water.

"It's how they get around," Trixi said. "They're not very good at swimming."

"They've got baby chicks too!" cried Ellie, watching a pingaloo mum with two little chicks who were waddling along together. They had much fluffier coats than the adults.

Summer spotted one of the chicks getting very close to the edge. "Oh, no!" she said anxiously. "I think he's going to...to..."

SPLASH! The chick fell into the water.

The mother bird started jumping up and down, flapping her wings and squawking. "Pingalooooo!" she shrieked. "Pingalooooo!"

The poor chick bobbed around in the water, struggling to stay afloat!

"We've got to save him!" said Ellie. She swished her tail and swam over to the struggling chick. Scooping him up in her hands, she placed him gently back on the ice floe.

"Pingaloo! Oh, thank you! Pingaloo!"
the mother squawked. A crowd of
pingaloos gathered round. They jumped
up and down on the spot all calling
"Pingaloo!" in grateful voices.

Summer, Jasmine and Trixi had now
caught up with Ellie. Rosa was mewing
in her bubble – she wanted to get out
and meet the birds!

One of the pingaloos came through
the crowd. He was a little taller than the
others with even bushier eyebrows.He
wore a golden crown on his head and
a warm cloak around his shoulders. He
clapped his flippers and the rest of the
pingaloos fell silent.

"I am king of the pingaloos!" he
declared. "Thank you, kind strangers,
for saving our chick. May I ask who

you are? You have
tails but I do not
believe you are
ice mermaids."

"Summer,
Ellie and
Jasmine are
humans,"
Trixi explained,
bowing to the
pingaloo king.
"They are Very
Important Friends of King Merry's. And I
am Trixibelle, a Royal Pixie."

"Pingalooooo!" the king squawked in
delight. "I'm delighted to meet you all."
He bobbed his head. "Now, please come
up and join us," he said, gesturing with
his flipper.

"Pingaloo!" the other birds cried
warmly. The girls scrambled up onto
the edge of the ice and Summer lifted
Rosa's bubble out of the water, but they
couldn't move around easily now they
had tails. The birds crowded round
them, nuzzling and nudging them with
their beaks.

"I think it might be time for us to stop being mermaids," Trixi said to the girls with a smile. She tapped her ring.

The pingaloos all squawked in surprise and backed away as sparkles swirled out and spun around the girls. A warm feeling rushed from the girls' heads to their toes and suddenly they were back to normal, dressed in their warm clothes again. Trixi gave a loud whistle and her magic leaf appeared by her side.

Rosa's bubble burst with a pop. She stared at the pingaloos as if she couldn't believe her eyes!

The girls stood up. Their legs felt a bit wobbly, but it was nice to be walking again!

"So, why are you here?" the king of the pingaloos asked.

"We're trying to find the magical Seal Keeper — she's keeper of kindness in the Secret Kingdom," explained Trixi. "We wanted to speak to the ice mermaids to see if they'd seen her, but they wouldn't let us in the palace."

The king shook his head sadly. "We don't know what's happened to the ice mermaids. They're normally so kind. They usually bring us yummy things to eat and help us teach our chicks to swim, but now they won't help us at all."

"That's because the seal's magic is mixed up. She's making everyone she comes across unkind instead of kind!" said Summer. "I don't suppose any of you have seen a little white seal pup swimming around?"

The pingaloos all shook their heads.

"The seal can't have come near the ice floe," Jasmine realised. "The pingaloos aren't being unkind."

SPLASH!

"Pingaloo!" a mother bird near the edge of the floe shrieked. Another chick had fallen in!

Ellie, Summer and Jasmine raced over. The little chick was flapping in the water, his eyes wide with fear. Jasmine kneeled down and tried to reach the chick but he was just too far away. If only she still had her tail she would have jumped into the icy water!

"Hang on to me, Ellie!" she said desperately. Ellie held onto Jasmine's waist. Jasmine stretched out further and further over the water and just managed to scoop up the wet baby. "Don't worry, you're safe," she soothed, putting him back down on the ice. His mother ran over gratefully. But then, almost immediately, another chick fell in!

Summer watched anxiously as Ellie and Jasmine fished him out too. What were they going to do? They couldn't stay with the pingaloos, they had to find the Seal Keeper. But if they left, lots more babies would fall into the sea! "Oh, what can we do?" she murmured to Rosa.

Rosa rubbed her head against Summer's cheek, the charms on her collar clinking. Summer saw that the

seal's golden heart-shaped charm was
glowing with a faint light. She could see
a few more words on it:

> "If you want to summon me
> From wherever I..."

"Ellie! Jasmine!" she called as they
fished the third chick out of the water.
"More words have appeared on the
charm! If we can make the rest of the
Seal Keeper's spell appear, we should be
able to summon her."

"You're right," said Jasmine with a big
smile. "We just have to keep on being
kind!"

"How about if we help the pingaloos
look after their chicks?" suggested Ellie.
"We could build them a playpen!"

"And I could conjure them up some fish. They must be hungry if the mermaids have decided not to help them find food," said Trixi.

Jasmine turned to the king who was listening to them talk, his head on one side. "Would that be all right, Your Majesty?"

"It would be most kind of you," said the king. "Pingalooooo!"

Summer started to round up the chicks while Jasmine and Ellie quickly started to build a playpen out of the ice and snow. Even Rosa tried to help by chasing after any chicks that got away from Summer and went too near the edge of the floe! Meanwhile, Trixi tapped her ring and conjured up a huge pile of fish for the pingaloos to eat.

All the pingaloos squawked in delight
and jumped up and down, crying,
"PINGALOOO!"

As Jasmine and Ellie finished the
pingaloo playpen, Summer checked the
charm on Rosa's collar. "More words
have appeared!" she cried.

*"If you want to summon me
From wherever I might be,
Jump up high..."*

She stopped. The words faded out mid-sentence. "Well, I guess we know we've got to jump up high," Summer said. She tried jumping up and down, but nothing happened.

"We'll have to do more kind things to make the rest of the spell appear," said Jasmine.

"Oh, no!" they heard Ellie cry. She was standing near the edge of the ice floe, staring out to sea. "Look over there, everyone!"

Summer and Jasmine stared. A spooky-looking yacht with black sails had

appeared on the horizon and it was
sailing quickly towards them. As it got
closer, they could make out a tall thin
woman with black frizzy hair standing at
the bow. She was holding a staff high in
the air and her eyes gleamed wickedly.

"It's Queen Malice!" Summer gasped.

Crash!

"What's Queen Malice doing here?"
cried Trixi.

"I don't know, but her yacht is heading
straight for Lady Frida's palace!" said
Jasmine.

The Storm Sprites sailing the yacht
flapped their bat-like wings and shrieked

in delight as the yacht gathered speed.

"Pingalooooo!" the pingaloos all
squawked anxiously.

"She's going to crash into the ice
mermaids' palace!" cried Ellie.

"What if any mermaids are close
by and get crushed or injured?" said
Summer in alarm, hugging Rosa close.

"We need to warn Lady Frida," said
Jasmine. She ran to the king. "Your
Majesty, please can you steer the ice floe
to the land so we can run and warn the
mermaids about the danger they're in?"

He nodded. "Of course. PINGALOO!"
he squawked to the pingaloos.

The pingaloos all raced to the edge of
the ice floe and picked up their paddles.
In no time at all, the ice floe was
skimming across the water like a giant

raft. The girls each grabbed a paddle
too, splashing the oars through the icy
water as fast as they could. Soon they
were almost at the iceberg.

"Pingaloo, pingaloo, PINGALOO!"
the pingaloos chanted as they expertly
turned the floe and stopped it beside the
ice. The girls jumped off.

"Thank you!" cried Jasmine. "It was lovely to meet you!"

The girls raced across the snow, their feet slipping and sliding. Trixi flew before them on her leaf. Summer found it hard to run with Rosa in her arms but she did her best. They had to warn the mermaids! Queen Malice's yacht was racing ever closer to the walls of the glittering ice palace.

As the girls reached the door, Trixi tapped her ring and called out a spell:

*"Bolts pull back and locks undo.
Now please let us all come through!"*

Sparkles hit the door and it flew open. The girls tumbled inside and found themselves in a huge hall. There was a

raised silver throne at one end and most
of the floor was taken up by a large
sunken swimming pool, lined with silver
mosaic tiles. Around the edge of the hall
were heavy curtains that blocked out
the sunlight from outside. A beautiful
mermaid was sitting on the throne.
She had long blonde hair held back
with a diamond tiara and her tail was
a shimmering green. In the swimming
pool were a crowd of other merpeople
– some male, some female – all with
long, swishy tails that glittered and
shone. None of them looked very happy
though. They had their arms folded
and weren't talking to each other. The
mermaid on the throne was scowling.

"Who are you?" she snapped,
outraged, as the girls skidded to a halt.

"How dare you burst into my palace!"

"Lady Frida! It's me, Trixi. King Merry's Royal Pixie," said Trixi, flying towards her and bowing.

Lady Frida frowned and flapped her hand. "Oh, go away, you silly little

thing. I'm not in the mood for visitors."

Jasmine hurried forward. The queen looked very cross but she had to say something. "Your Majesty, we're not here just to visit — we're here to warn you that Queen Malice is coming. She's heading straight for your palace in a huge yacht!"

Lady Frida looked alarmed. "Queen Malice is coming here? Whatever for?"

"We don't know," said Jasmine. "But we had to tell you!"

"Open the curtains!" commanded Lady Frida, diving into the pool and swimming to the window. "Let me see!"

One of the mermaids pulled a golden cord. The curtains swept back to reveal a huge window with a balcony and a stunning view of the ocean. The

merpeople all cried out as they saw
Queen Malice's yacht hurtling across the
waves towards them.

Ellie, Summer and Jasmine ran to the
window and opened it. The yacht was
now very close and the girls could see
that the silly sprites had *completely* lost
control of steering it! The sprite at the
wheel of the yacht was covering his face
with his hands!

Queen Malice wasn't laughing any
more. She looked worried and was

shrieking at the Storm Sprites. "Slow down, you fools! We're going to crash!" She started backing away from the front of the yacht. "SLOW DOWN!"

CRASH!

The whole palace shook as the yacht crashed into its icy walls. It stayed there, wedged into the ice. Ellie, Summer and Jasmine grabbed each other as the ice all around them groaned and creaked.

The Storm Sprites had to grab the sails and railings to stop themselves being thrown over the side of the yacht. Queen Malice had been knocked backwards. She scrambled up, looking furious.

"You snowflake-brained, flappy-winged idiots! You almost destroyed the Thunder Yacht *and* drowned me!" She shook her staff at the sprites and they cowered in front of her. "Fools!"

Queen Malice shook back her mane of black hair and stalked to the front of the yacht. She looked up at the girls standing in the window.

"You!" she hissed, pointing her staff. "You always interfere, don't you? Well, I'm here to stop you finding the Seal Keeper. I want everyone in this kingdom to be mean and unkind!"

"We won't let you do that!" cried Jasmine fiercely.

"No way!" shouted Ellie.

"Oh, really," the queen jeered. "Well, we'll see about that." She pointed her staff at them and started to hiss a spell.

"With magic dark, I curse you now...

ARGH!" She screamed suddenly as a shimmering whale leaped out of the ocean, sending a spray of water raining down on her, before diving back into the sea with a huge splash. Queen Malice screamed in fury, water dripping off her pointed nose and chin.

"Was that Arva?" gasped Summer.

Ellie nodded. "I think it was!"

Just then, another amazing shimmering whale leaped out of the water, but this one was enormous!

"It's Arva's mum!" cried Jasmine.

The mother whale leaped over the

Thunder Yacht and dived back into the water, sending a huge wave crashing over the Storm Sprites and Queen Malice. The wave was strong enough to free the boat from the ice. It bobbed backwards away from the palace, making the queen fall over again.

The girls and the merpeople started to giggle.

Queen Malice clawed herself upright using the side of the yacht. She was soaking! "You'll be sorry for this!" she howled. She started to raise her staff again but just then a snowball flew through the air from the right and hit her on the head. Another followed, and another. Queen Malice had to dance around to avoid the snowballs, ducking and dodging all over the place!

"It's the pingaloos!" Ellie realised. The pingaloos were dancing up and down on their ice floe, grabbing flipper loads of snow and flinging snowballs through the air, bombarding the queen and the Storm Sprites. Even the babies were joining in!

"Ow!" the Storm Sprites screeched.

"My wings!"

"My head!"

"My bottom!"

"PINGALOOOOO!" squawked the pingaloos, throwing even more snowballs at the yacht.

Queen Malice batted away the snowballs with her staff. "Argh!" she shouted to the Storm Sprites. "Retreat to a safe distance!"

The Storm Sprites steered the yacht backwards and it began to sail away. The pingaloos cheered and whooped, and the two whales popped their heads out of the water to blow fountains of water up from their blow-holes in triumph.

"Oh, thank you!" Summer cried to the pingaloos and the whales.

"It's our pleasure!" bellowed Arva's mum. "You were so kind to us earlier!"

"But what about the palace walls?" said Jasmine. "They're badly damaged." She went out onto the balcony to look more closely at the mess the ship had made. But just then, a loud roar echoed across the snowy plains. She turned and saw the huge figure of an ice giant stomping towards the palace, his massive stride covering the ground quickly. He looked very cross!

Oh, no! Jasmine caught her breath. They might have fought off Queen Malice, but it looked like another danger was heading straight towards them!

Helping Hands

"The ice giant is coming!" Jasmine cried.

"Maybe the Seal Keeper went near him and turned him mean, too!" said Ellie in dismay. "Trixi, can you do something to calm him down?" she asked desperately.

"He's much too strong for my magic to stop," gasped Trixi. "What are we going to do?"

Summer hurried onto the balcony beside Jasmine. "He's really close now!" She could hear him roaring! What was

he saying? Summer tried to make out
the words.

"I'LL GET YOU..."

Summer gulped. That didn't sound
good!

"I'LL TEACH YOU A LESSON
YOU WON'T FORGET, QUEEN
MALICE!"

Queen Malice? Summer blinked. Had
she heard that right? The giant roared
again.

"HOW DARE YOU DAMAGE MY
FRIEND'S PALACE!"

Summer caught her breath. The ice
giant wasn't cross with *them*. He was
cross with Queen Malice!

Queen Malice's yacht had stopped
a little way away from the palace but
it soon sped off as the ice giant came

closer – the cowardly queen wasn't brave
enough to face him!

Lady Frida threw up her arms. "People
shouting! People crashing yachts into my
palace! People coming in when they're
not wanted! I've had enough!" She gave
an angry scream and dived down into
the dark waters below the palace. The
other merpeople followed her in a huff.

"Let's go and see the ice giant,"
said Ellie.

Trixi and the three girls raced out of
the palace and onto the icy plains. The
ice giant had stopped beside the sea's
edge and was shaking his club. He was
absolutely enormous!

"What's going on here?" bellowed the
ice giant. "I saw Queen Malice crash

into Lady Frida's palace in that Thunder
Yacht of hers. Where is she now?"

"She's gone," said Ellie. "The pingaloos
and the whales helped chase her off."

The pingaloos jumped up and down
on the ice floe and the whales shot water
happily out of their blowholes.

"Then Queen Malice saw you coming
and fled," said Jasmine.

The ice giant frowned. "Where's my friend, Lady Frida?"

"She went underwater with the rest of the ice mermaids," said Ellie. "She's not being very friendly today, I'm afraid."

"It's all Queen Malice's fault," said Jasmine. "It started at King Merry's palace." She explained about the curse Queen Malice had put on the Animal Keepers. "We're going to find them and break the curse," she finished.

"But that's the reason why Lady Frida isn't being her normal self," said Summer. "The Seal Keeper has made all the ice mermaids unkind."

"Poor Lady Frida," the ice giant said, shaking his head. "And her palace is damaged too. I'll see if I can help fix things."

"That would be great!" said Jasmine, delighted. "We can help clear up too."

"And us!" squawked the pingaloos. They jumped off the ice floe and came waddling round to the girls.

The ice giant expertly climbed up the side of the palace and began to touch the broken walls with his huge hands. Everywhere he touched new ice appeared, layer after layer, repairing the damage until the walls sparkled in the sunshine again.

Meanwhile, the girls and the pingaloos hurried about picking up the chunks of ice that were scattered on the snow around the palace. They pushed them all into the water. The merpeople surfaced and watched what was happening from a distance.

When all the bits of ice had gone, the pingaloos brushed the snow perfectly smooth with their wings. Even Rosa helped by brushing it with her tail!

"Finished!" said the ice giant, standing back to look at the palace walls, which were shining and beautiful again.

"We've fixed all the damage!" cried Ellie, hugging Jasmine.

"We've done more than that," gasped Summer, crouching down by Rosa. "Look!" She unclipped the charm from Rosa's collar. "The whole summoning spell has appeared!" She read it out:

"If you want to summon me
From wherever I might be,
Jump up high, hand in hand,
And say my name as you land!"

"What are we waiting for?" said Ellie with a grin. Summer put Rosa down and held hands with Ellie and Jasmine.

"One, two, three!" cried Jasmine.

They all jumped up. As they landed, they called out, "Seal Keeper!"

There was a bright flash and a little white seal appeared on the ice. Her fur

was fluffy and she had big dark eyes. Her
whiskers twitched as she looked round
at them and then she saw the charm in
Summer's hands. She moved across the
snow, making a sad honking sound.

She stopped and looked hopefully at
Summer, her long whiskers trembling.

Summer understood immediately what
she wanted. "Yes. You can have it
back." She crouched down and clipped
the charm to the seal's
collar. There was a bright
flash of silver and the
seal somersaulted in
delight, then stood
up on her tail and
clapped her flippers
together. She looked
so much happier!

She flapped over to Summer, Jasmine and Ellie giving them all seal cuddles. Even the ice giant got a snuffly seal kiss!

The girls felt so warm and happy. Jasmine ran over and hugged Ellie and Summer. "You two are the best friends ever!"

"And you too!" said Ellie, her eyes shining.

"I'm so glad we've broken the spell," said Summer. Rosa rubbed her head against Summer's cheek, purring in agreement.

"My friends!" A silvery voice carried across the water. It was Lady Frida. She swam over to them, her eyes anxious. "Thank you so much for repairing the damage to my palace." The other merpeople joined her and nodded.

"I don't know what's been the matter with us," said Lady Frida, looking embarrassed and ashamed. "I know we've been horrible to everyone. I'm so very sorry."

"Please don't feel bad," said Jasmine. "It was because of Queen Malice's spell." She quickly explained what had happened.

Lady Frida gasped. "That's dreadful!" She looked around. "I'm so sorry we have been mean," she said, looking at the pingaloos and the whales. The other merpeople started to apologise too, stroking Arva and hugging the pingaloos.

"At least you're back to normal now," said Ellie. "And so is the Seal Keeper!"

The white seal honked loudly. She gave them a big open-mouthed smile and then with a wave of her flipper she dived into the water.

"She'll spread kindness around the rest of the Secret Kingdom now," said Trixi in delight. "Queen Malice's curse on her has been broken."

"This calls for a celebration!" cried Lady Frida. "I shall organise a mermaid picnic here on the rocks for everyone!"

★

The picnic was amazing. The merpeople carried huge trays of food out of the castle onto the snow, where the girls laid them out on blankets of soft seaweed.

There were iced biscuits in the shape of dolphins, big bowls of rainbow-coloured ice cream with each stripe a different flavour, jugs of iced fruit punch and little sugar starfish to eat. At the centre of the feast was a ten-tiered ice cream cake with a sugar mermaid on the top. The ice giant used his club to make a brilliant ice slide for the girls and the pingaloos to play on and Trixi conjured up lots of yummy fishy treats for Rosa and the pingaloos – *and* some extra-specially big fishy treats for the whales!

Soon they were all eating, talking,

laughing and playing. Afterwards, the mermaids and whales played tag in the sea while the girls and the pingaloos raced down the ice slide. Rosa played gently with the pingaloo chicks, letting them climb all over her and chase her in and out of their igloo homes. It was the most wonderful picnic the girls had ever been to!

Finally, it was time for the girls to go home. "We'll send you another message just as soon as we work out where the other Keepers are," said Trixi. "Thank you and see you soon!"

"Bye, everyone!" cried Ellie, Summer and Jasmine together.

Trixi tapped her ring and the girls were whisked away, tumbling over and over until they landed safely back in Summer's bedroom. Summer checked the clock. As usual, no time had passed in the real world while they had been gone. She could still hear her brothers playing outside on the climbing frame. It was very strange to be back in her cozy bedroom after being surrounded by ice and snow!

"Wow!" Jasmine pushed a hand

through her hair. "What an adventure!"

Rosa shook herself and hopped back up onto Summer's bed. She curled up and yawned, her tail twitching. "I wonder if she'll dream of pingaloos tonight," said Summer with a smile.

Ellie jumped to her feet. "I don't feel tired at all."

"Neither do I," said Jasmine. "In fact, I feel ready for another adventure already!"

Summer giggled and linked arms with her friends. "We'll always be ready for another adventure in the Secret Kingdom!"

In the next Secret Kingdom adventure, Ellie, Summer and Jasmine must find the

Glitter Bird

Read on for a sneak peek...

A Message From Trixi

"Ready?" asked Jasmine Smith.

"You bet!" said her best friends Ellie Macdonald and Summer Hammond together. It was half term and the three girls were in Summer's bedroom. Jasmine had brought a DVD, *Animal Acrobats*, for them to watch because it was too rainy to play outside.

"Here goes then," Jasmine said, flicking back her long dark hair. She pressed play on the DVD player and sat down on Summer's bed. "I love this film, it's really funny. Especially the bit where the baby owls are learning to fly."

Summer smiled dreamily and stroked her cute little black cat, Rosa, who was curled up beside her on the bed. "I love it when we get to fly in the Secret Kingdom. It's such fun!"

Ellie wrinkled her nose. "I don't," she said. "I prefer staying on the ground, thanks! But I *do* love going to the Secret Kingdom." She smiled, feeling a thrill of excitement as she thought about the amazing secret they all shared.

The girls looked after a magic box that could whisk them off to a wonderful, enchanted land, filled with mermaids, unicorns and other amazing creatures. Summer, Jasmine and Ellie were Very Important Friends of the magical kingdom, and went there every time kind King Merry needed help to keep the land safe from his evil sister, Queen Malice.

Ellie kneeled down by the bed and tickled Rosa. Purring, the little cat rolled over and batted her fingers playfully. The movement set two gold charms on her collar jingling. One was shaped like a flower and the other like a crown.

"I wish we could go back to the Secret Kingdom right now," said Ellie, touching the charms gently. "We need to return these charms to the last two Animal Keepers."

A few days ago, King Merry had

summoned the four Animal Keepers from their shield with ancient magic. These magical creatures – a puppy, a seal, a bird and a lion – came out of the shield once every hundred years and travelled through the Secret Kingdom for one week, spreading fun, kindness, friendship and bravery all around the land. But mean Queen Malice had cast a horrible spell, meaning that they now brought the opposite wherever they went – misery, squabbling, meanness and cowardice!

"I'm sure Trixi will send us a message soon," Summer said. Their friend Trixibelle was a Royal Pixie. She worked for King Merry and used the Magic Box to get in touch with the girls whenever help was needed in the Secret Kingdom.

The girls had spent lots of their half term holiday at Summer's house because they needed to take Rosa with them next time they went to the Secret Kingdom.

In their first adventure with the Puppy Keeper, Summer, Ellie and Jasmine had attached the four Animal Keepers' charms onto Rosa's collar to keep them safe. Once the charms were returned to each Animal Keeper, Queen Malice's spell would be broken!

Read

Glitter Bird

to find out what happens next!

Have you read all the books in Series Four?

Meet the magical Animal Keepers of the Secret Kingdom, who spread fun, friendship, kindness and bravery throughout the land!

Secret Kingdom

Be in on the secret... Discover the first enchanting series!

Series 1

When Jasmine, Summer and Ellie discover the magical land of the Secret Kingdom, a whole world of adventure awaits!

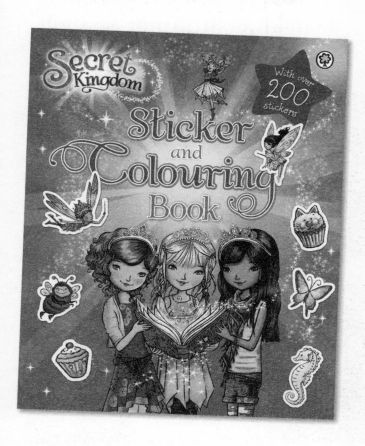

The magical world of Secret Kingdom
comes to life with this gorgeous sticker and
colouring book. Out now!

Look out for the next sparkling summer special!

Join the girls on a special pixie-sized adventure!

Available
June 2014

Secret Kingdom

Don't miss the next amazing series!

It's Ellie, Summer and Jasmine's most
important adventure yet... Queen Malice has
taken over the Secret Kingdom! The girls must
find four magic jewels to make King Merry
a new crown and return him to the throne –
but where in the kingdom can the gems be?

Available
August 2014

Secret Kingdom Shield Competition!

Can you help best friends Ellie, Summer and Jasmine solve the riddles?

At the back of each Secret Kingdom adventure in this set (books 19-22) is a different riddle for you to solve. The answers are all connected to a character featured in this set of Secret Kingdom books.

Here's how you enter the competition:

✽ Read and solve the riddle on the page opposite
✽ Once you think you know the answer, go to
www.secretkingdombooks.com
to print out the special shield activity sheet
✽ Draw the animal that you think is the answer
to the riddle on the shield
✽ Once you've drawn all four correct answers,
send your entry into us!

The lucky winners will receive a bumper Secret Kingdom goody bag full of treats and activities.

Please send entries to:
Secret Kingdom Shield Competition
Orchard Books, 338 Euston Road, London, NW1 3BH

Don't forget to add your name and address.

Good luck!

Closing date: 31st October 2014

Riddle two

Causing trouble in the Snowy Seas

This silvery Keeper needs your help, please!

The answer is

....

Secret Kingdom

A magical world of
friendship and fun!

Join the Secret Kingdom Club at

www.secretkingdombooks.com

and enjoy games, sneak peeks and lots more!

You'll find great activities, competitions, stories
and games, plus a special newsletter for
Secret Kingdom friends!